PUDDING BAG SCHOOL

A STRONG SMELL OF Magic

PUDDING BAG SCHOOL

A STRONG SMELL OF MAGIC

Hilary McKay

Illustrated by
David Melling

Hodder
Children's
Books

a division of Hodder Headline Limited

First published in Great Britain in 1999
by Hodder Children's Books

This edition published in 2003 by Hodder Children's Books

A Catalogue record for this book is available from
the British Library

ISBN 0 340 87751 0

Typeset in Palatino by Avon DataSet Ltd,
Bidford-on-Avon, Warwickshire

Printed and bound in Great Britain by
Clays Ltd., St Ives plc, Bungay, Suffolk

Hodder Children's Books
a division of Hodder Headline Limited
338 Euston Road
London NW1 3BH

CHAPTER ONE

Class 4b, Pudding Bag School

Class 4b, Pudding Bag School, were taught to recognise the smell of magic by their teacher, Miss Gilhoolie. She thought it was very important.

Most of the parents of the children at Pudding Bag School did not quite know what to make of Miss Gilhoolie. She seemed too cheerful for a teacher, and too pretty. She was very fond of diamonds (the bigger the better) and she wore them every day by the dozen. Her beetle-shiny, bright green Ferrari also caused comments, and so did the way she could whistle through her fingers, and so did her short, tight skirts.

On the other hand, said the parents fairly,

1

the children seemed to learn an awful lot from her, and they brought home vast quantities of homework which was always a good sign. Also they were all very eager to get to school each day. In fact since Miss Gilhoolie took over they never had the early morning stomach aches and sicknesses that had bothered them in the past. The general opinion was that Miss Gilhoolie would be a very good teacher once she had settled down and stopped giving the children ideas.

Class 4b liked her just the way she was.

'She may be bossy,' said Dougal McDougal. 'But at least she's not boring!'

Dougal McDougal was ten years old. He had red hair and lots of ideas of his own, not all of them good. His best friend was Simon Percy. Simon also had ideas – less than Dougal, but usually better. Simon was much quieter than Dougal, but then so was everyone else in Class 4b.

There were two classes of ten year olds in Pudding Bag School: 4a and 4b.

'4b is the brainy ones class,' said Dougal McDougal.

'Rubbish!' said Miss Gilhoolie, sparkling with diamonds as usual, and (also as usual) putting up with no nonsense from Dougal McDougal. 'Class 4b are perfectly ordinary! Rather behind if anything. You missed such a lot last term.'

Dougal grinned, but did not reply. He knew, and Miss Gilhoolie knew he knew, that Class 4b were not perfectly ordinary. They had stopped being ordinary two terms ago, when Miss Gilhoolie came.

It was Class 4b who, the Autumn before, had built the firework-propelled rocket that blasted their frightful headmaster into deepest space. When London had the coldest February ever and the whole population was evacuated by helicopter to the sunny North, it was Class 4b who were left behind. They had escaped with the help of the school cat and had been National News for a day or two but Miss Gilhoolie had not been impressed.

'Fancy being snowed up in school for all

that time and none of you doing the least bit of work!' she had complained when she finally got them back. 'You will have to make up for it now!'

Class 4b had been making up for it ever since, but they did not mind very much. Miss Gilhoolie had a way of making most things interesting. Science, for example, included pop corn making and panning for gold. The Geography Project survey of the local neighbourhood was done by hot air balloon. On their summer term school trip, when all the other classes were going to visit zoos and adventure playgrounds and open air theatres, Class 4b were taken to learn to recognise the smell of magic.

'Everybody has *smelt* it,' Miss Gilhoolie told Class 4b the day before they were to set off. 'But most people do not recognise it and that is a waste because it is there for a reason.'

'What reason?' asked Madeline Brown.

'To remind you to enjoy yourself,' said Miss Gilhoolie. 'Or to warn you not to meddle. Or both. Depending on how strong it is.'

4

'But how are *we* going to find magic to smell?' asked Samantha Freebody. 'Unless Miss Gilhoolie can do magic. *Can* you do magic, Miss Gilhoolie?'

'Really Samantha, do I look like a witch?' demanded Miss Gilhoolie, and then just as Samantha was about to reply 'Yes, very much,' went on,

'Of course, I can't conjure up the *exact* smell of *real* magic, but what I have arranged for you is a very good second best. Copy down this recipe in the backs of your Science and Technology books.'

The recipe was:

One large bottle of the *most* expensive French perfume

One large healthy hedgehog

One large barrow-load of freshly fallen snow (preferably taken from a pine forest)

One boot cupboard full of well worn old boots

A fresh west wind off the sea

'Those are the standard ingredients,' said Miss Gilhoolie, 'and anything else is fiddle-faddle! Yes, Simon dear?'

'Does it hurt the hedgehog?'

'Of course not,' said Miss Gilhoolie. 'You merely *add* the hedgehog *to* the boots, wait two minutes to allow the smell to infuse, *pile* in the snow (it will not bother the hedgehog at all as long as we brush it off again before it melts), *pour* on the perfume, open all the windows so that the wind blows through, and there you are!'

'I should think,' remarked Madeline Brown, who was very clever, 'that you must have to be very quick. Otherwise, won't the snow melt and the hedgehog run away and the boots and the perfume get too strong to bear?'

'Timing is absolutely critical,' agreed Miss Gilhoolie. 'Now, it is a long way from here to a suitable coast with a reliable west wind from the sea, so I am afraid the coach will not be able to wait for anyone who is late tomorrow. I have hired an understanding fisherman's cottage, and the snow is being flown in from Norway by a friend of mine and will reach us at twelve o'clock. We will leave school at eight in the morning and there should just be time for one good sniff each before we have to come back. Bring packed lunches, travel sickness pills and no fizzy drinks please! Any more questions?'

'It seems an awful lot of trouble,' said Samantha Freebody.

'It will be worth it,' said Miss Gilhoolie.

Just after twelve o'clock the next day Class 4b, rather stiff after their three and a half hour coach ride, filed one by one into the understanding fisherman's cottage, stuck their heads into the boot cupboard where the ingredients had been mixed, breathed deeply, said Oh Miss Gilhoolie! breathed again, and then filed out and back onto the coach for the long journey home. And they thought that it had been worth it.

'I've smelt that smell before,' said Madeline

in class the following morning. 'Not strong like that was yesterday, sometimes hardly so you'd notice at all, but lots and lots of times.'

'Everyone has,' agreed Miss Gilhoolie. 'They just don't recognise it. They say things like, 'You really should feel the air tonight,' or 'What's somebody cooking?' or, 'How that takes me back!' They know there is something special about, but hardly anyone can give it a name.'

'Magic,' said Madeline.

'Yes, magic,' agreed Miss Gilhoolie. 'To be enjoyed but never meddled with! Write that down in the back of your Science and Technology books too, and then rule a *neat* line underneath. Hands down everyone! No more questions!'

Despite the fact that everyone would have been happy to discuss the subject all morning, Class 4b did as they'd been told. They knew by now that Miss Gilhoolie always grew rather impatient when she was asked for too many explanations. Also she seemed to have caught a very bad cold.

For a day or two people became very interested in tracking down things that smelt of magic. They went around constantly sniffing and comparing notes.

'Books,' said Simon Percy. 'It comes out of books.'

'Rain on the pavements when the weather's been dry,' said Charlotte.

'The dressing up box,' said someone else.

'Stones.'

'Tents.'

'The basement smells of it sometimes,' said Dougal. 'And I smelt it quite strongly coming out of the sweetshop once, the day after our rocket went up.'

'It didn't *go* up,' said Madeline. 'You *fired* it!'

'I've said sorry,' said Dougal. 'I've said sorry loads of times, Madeline Brown! I didn't know you were in it!'

'Miss Gilhoolie smells of magic sometimes,' remarked Simon dreamily, ignoring them both.

'She doesn't today though,' said Emma, Charlotte's twin. 'She smells of cough sweets. Cough sweets, sore throat sweets, and menthol inhaler.'

'I noticed that hedgehog was sneezing,' said Dougal, rather severely. 'Miss Gilhoolie needn't bother getting ill now! It's the Summer Fair next week and our class still hasn't thought of anything to do. 4a are having a Bouncy Castle! I bet they win the Special Class Prize!'

The Special Class Prize was to be awarded to the form that made the most money at the Summer Fair. Nobody but the governors knew what it was to be, and that made it even more desirable. Class 4a, who were great rivals of 4b, were behaving as if they'd won it already. They were a bossy lot. Long ago they had nicknamed 4b the Scruffs and Nutters, and no matter how many times Dougal McDougal fought them, they persisted in calling themselves the Brainy Ones class. They laughed unkindly at Brave Sir Lancelot, Class 4b's adopted lucky mascot. Brave Sir Lancelot was a rather mangy moose belonging to Miss Gilhoolie. He spent his time tethered at the furthest corners of the school playing field, keeping down the grass. He was an uninteresting animal and never smelt remotely magical, but even so he did not deserve to be laughed at. Madeline looked across to where he stood, morosely drooling dandelion juice down his bony chest. How lucky they were, she thought, to have the sort of teacher who would keep a moose for a pet, and she said loyally,

'Miss Gilhoolie is bound to think of something much better than a bouncy castle!'

Miss Gilhoolie refused to think of anything. She held her head in both hands and groaned as she gave out words for the afternoon spelling test. She covered her ears at Dougal McDougal's persistent explanations of the need for something more exciting than a bouncy castle.

'I dow know wob on earf your talbing abow!' she told Madeline, when Madeline tried to help Dougal. 'Wob on earf is a Subber Fair?'

Many people began to explain what on earth a summer fair was then, but Miss Gilhoolie exclaimed,

'Dow'n tell me, dow'n tell me!' and flapped them away and sneezed. Emma was right, she did not smell the least bit magicky.

'Messing about with snow and sneezing hedgehogs *just* when the school fair is coming up!' said Dougal, very crossly as he walked home with Madeline and Simon that night.

'Perhaps she'll be better in the morning,' said Madeline.

Miss Gilhoolie was worse in the morning. She did not come to school at all. Instead she sent in messages for Class 4b, a list of work as long as a banner and instructions on the care of the moose. The work was given out by various distracted teachers, rushing to and fro between their own classes and Class 4b. The instructions on the care of the moose were carried out by Class 4b themselves. Sir Lancelot became a sort of meeting point, or grumbling point, as Simon Percy remarked.

'I've just heard that 4a are having a candy floss stall as well,' reported Samantha Freebody to her fellow grumblers at lunchtime. 'One of their dads is sorting it out.'

There was deep groaning among Class 4b.

'They said 'Poor old Scruffs and Nutters' when they noticed me listening to them,' continued Samantha. 'And they said why don't we have Pin The Tail On The Donkey and use Sir Lancelot for the donkey.'

'They think they're so funny!' said Dougal bitterly. 'Mind what you're doing with that bucket Madeline! That was nearly my eye!'

'He joggled me,' said Madeline, mixing up rolled oats with moose nuts as instructed by Miss Gilhoolie while Sir Lancelot fidgeted with impatience. 'Do you think moose nuts smell a bit magicky?'

'Who cares if they do?' asked Dougal. 'A bouncy castle *and* a candy floss stall and we haven't got anything! Bother Miss Gilhoolie, messing about with snow and sneezing hedgehogs in all that wind! No wonder she's ill! She'd better be back tomorrow!'

Miss Gilhoolie was not back. She was in hospital, the terrible cold having gone to her chest. From her hospital bed she sent in more work lists, rolled oats, and moose nuts, and enough homework to last till the end of the week. Hot on the heels of the homework lists came the news that two of Class 4a's mothers had offered to organise a balloon race with real helium balloons.

'Balloons *and* a bouncy castle *and* a candy floss stall!' moaned Dougal McDougal. 'And we still haven't anything organised!'

The flying, distracted teachers from other

classes were no help at all. They suggested a book stall (if enough books could be collected), a Guess The Weight Of The Cake competition (if a cake could be got hold of), a white elephant stall, or helping the Infants with their Lucky Dip. Class 4a suggested rocket trips, sleigh rides and Spot The Flea on the Moose and added smugly that three of their dads had agreed to run a hot dog and hamburger stand.

'Why can't our parents do anything useful?' said Dougal McDougal.

The reason for this was quite simple. Class 4a's parents were things like doctors, computer salesmen, and professional golfers. Doctors, computer salesmen, professional golfers and the like could always get time off. Class 4b's parents were all things like bus drivers and firemen and mad professors, the sort of people who are busy all the time and cannot take afternoons away to help at school summer fairs. Madeline explained this to Dougal as she flea-powdered Sir Lancelot after school that day. Sir Lancelot seemed to need this treatment so often that The Spot the Flea competition suggested by Class 4a would undoubtably have been a huge success, had it not been so unkind.

'There's not a single useful parent in our whole class,' said Madeline, powdering away.

'Then Miss Gilhoolie must be *made* to help!' said Dougal firmly. 'I shall go and see her!'

'But she's in hospital,' said Madeline.

'Then I shall go and see her in hospital,' said Dougal McDougal.

CHAPTER TWO

Dougal in Disguise

Samantha Freebody said that she was quite, quite sure that Dougal would not be allowed to go and see Miss Gilhoolie in hospital. It was not often that people agreed with Samantha, but this time they did.

'It's not as if you were a friend or relation,' pointed out Charlotte.

'It's not as if you were going to be kind,' said Emma.

'It's not as if you were grown up,' said Samuel Moon.

Dougal said of course he was a friend, Miss Gilhoolie was very fond of him, and of course he was going to be kind. Think how upset she would be if Class 4a won the

Special Class Prize.

'And I may not be grown up but I'm bigger than you are anyway, Samuel Moon!' he told Samuel. 'I thought you'd be on my side!'

'Anyway, you can't visit her, you don't know which hospital she's in,' said Samuel.

It was very easy to find out which hospital Miss Gilhoolie had been sent to. Dougal simply asked the school secretary. She was new that term and did not know Dougal very well and she assumed he wanted to send a Get Well card.

'Very kind of you, dear,' she remarked as she wrote down the address, and she thought what a nice child he looked, with his chestnut hair and his freckles and his innocent, shining eyes.

'Thank you,' said Dougal, smiling at her as if butter wouldn't melt in his mouth, and he went off to boast of his cunning to the rest of Class 4b, gathered as usual in a grumbling huddle around Sir Lancelot the Brave.

'Guess what this is!' he said, waving the slip of paper under Samuel's nose, and without waiting for a reply, 'Miss Gilhoolie's hospital's address! What *are* you all eating?'

'Moose nuts,' replied Simon Percy. 'How did you find that, then?'

'Office,' said Dougal. 'That new secretary gave it to me. What do they taste like, moose nuts?'

'Pencil sharpenings. Mixed with treacle. Are you really going to try and visit her then?'

' 'Course I am,' replied Dougal. 'Someone's got to help us with the School Summer Fair. I'll tell her what 4a are doing and ask her if she can think of something really good for us. Give me a moose nut someone!'

Simon handed him a moose nut and volunteered to come with him to visit Miss Gilhoolie.

Dougal chewed and swallowed and choked and spluttered and said they might have warned him.

'Crikey, they're disgusting!' he added. 'No wonder Sir Lancelot looks like he does.'

'You swallowed yours too quickly,' said Samuel Moon. 'They're all right if you chew

them for ages and ages like chewing gum.
Are you going to let Simon go with you
then?'

'I don't know,' said Dougal. 'I've been
thinking about what you said about not being
grown up and you might be right. So I don't
know if Simon can come.'

'I should think if they'll let in you, they'll
let in Simon.'

'Yes, but I shan't *be* me,' said Dougal. 'I shall
go in disguise! Could you get me one of your
Dad's white coats Madeline, do you think?'

'I suppose so,' agreed Madeline, whose father was a mad professor and owned many white coats. 'But what are you going to be disguised as?'

'A doctor of course!'

'You're not tall enough!'

'A *short* doctor then,' said Dougal. 'There's loads of short doctors! A very short doctor in a white coat and I thought I'd put red paint blood on it to make it look more real.'

'Oh, let me come as well,' begged Simon Percy, enchanted at this vision. 'Madeline could get a white coat for me too, couldn't you Madeline?'

Madeline said rather doubtfully that she thought perhaps she could, but Dougal objected.

'Two very short doctors would be much too many!'

'You just said there were loads of them!' protested Simon.

'Yes, but I don't suppose they go around together! Everyone would notice two very short doctors together!'

Simon thought this might very well be true. Also he knew from long experience what a waste of time it was, trying to argue with Dougal McDougal. Instead he asked,

'Can I come with you and wait outside then?'

'Of course,' said Dougal generously. 'And you can help me get ready too if you like.'

'We could use my new face paints to paint your face a proper doctorish colour,' suggested Simon. 'Greyish, they usually are.'

'And greenish,' said Madeline.

'Greenish and purpleish, like Sir Lancelot's tongue,' said Charlotte, and several people immediately agreed.

'It's going to look awful,' said Samantha Freebody.

'It's going to look perfect,' said Dougal.

The disguising was done in Simon's bedroom after school that afternoon, and the result was quite amazing. Dougal's face was coloured a doctorish greenish purpleish grey and they put white streaks in his hair. Red face paint

splashed on the wrists and front of Madeline's father's white coat looked impressively gory.

'I think perhaps I look more like a surgeon than an ordinary doctor,' remarked Dougal, admiring himself in the mirror.

'Perhaps you do,' agreed Simon, and made him a badge with his badge making kit.

EMERGENCY HEART SURGEON read the badge.

'Now all you need is doctorish things in your pockets,' said Simon.

That was easily done. The kitchen and the bathroom and the tool shed in the garden were ransacked for suitable instruments. Soon an array of vegetable knives, potato peelers, pliers, chisels and sticking plasters filled Dougal's pockets. The duster that had been used to mop up some spilt red face paint added a perfect finishing touch.

'But how are we going to get to the hospital?' asked Simon. 'You can't go on a bus dressed like that!'

'We'll walk then. It's not that far. Anyway, I could cover most of it up if you could find something that would do.'

The only things that Simon could think of were his father's raincoat and his mother's umbrella. These were borrowed and added to the disguise so that when they set out there was nothing to be seen of the Emergency Heart Surgeon at all. Even so he was an unusual sight.

'Are people noticing me?' he asked from under the umbrella as they walked along.

'Yes.'

'Many?'

'Thousands. I suppose it's the umbrella. It's such a dry day.'

'Oh well,' said Dougal, 'I expect it will be worth it.'

All the same he was relieved when they arrived at the huge glass doors of the hospital. There he handed the coat and umbrella over to Simon, smoothed his blood-stained heart surgeon's cuffs and marched boldly through the entrance.

Dougal had not known quite what to expect inside the hospital. He had thought pessimistically that he might be chased straight back out again, and he had thought optimistically that he might be invited to operate, but it had never crossed his mind that no one would notice him at all. Yet that is what happened. A group of visitors were hovering around a large plan of the building. They made room for him to look too, without even glancing up. He found Miss Gilhoolie's ward on the plan and as he made his way towards it a man in a similar white coat nodded briefly but did not pause. A fat nurse in a blue uniform remarked to a giggling friend that the students seemed to get younger every year, but made no other comment. It was all so easy that by the time Dougal reached the ward he was looking for he was bouncing with confidence. He marched through the double doors with a rattle of knives and scissors. Then he stood in the middle of the room pushing up his too long, gore splattered sleeves and looked speculatively around.

This time he *was* noticed. Two old ladies

burst into loud wheezy laughter and a third leapt from her bed and ran shrieking down the corridor. A nurse scuttled after her, and another seized Dougal. She dropped him a moment later, having been stabbed by a potato peeler, giving Dougal a chance to announce,

'I've come to see Miss Gilhoolie!'

From a curtained off corner of the room there came a very loud groan.

'Come to see Miss Gilhoolie?' repeated the nurse and from behind the curtains a hoarse croaky voice called,

'It's all right nurse. He is perfectly harmless! It's only Dougal McDougal.'

'Miss Gilhoolie!' cried Dougal, dashing to the curtains and pulling them aside, and there was Miss Gilhoolie. She was propped up by pillows and surrounded by medicine bottles, tissue boxes, bouquets of flowers and quantities of loose diamonds. She looked very pale and very ill and very, very cross.

'Dougal McDougal,' she said, weakly but furiously. 'What do you think you are doing?'

Dougal noticed the furiousness, but he also noticed the weakness and so was not alarmed. He plumped himself down on the end of the bed, sniffed happily at the smell of magic that was arising from the flowers and the diamonds, and began a long and indignant account of the problems of Class 4b, Pudding Bag School, what with the Summer Fair coming up, and their teacher in bed, and Class 4a so rude and gloating, and not a useful parent between them.

After a while Miss Gilhoolie closed her eyes.

'Don't go to sleep!' said Dougal, and started again.

'Summer fair,' Miss Gilhoolie heard, repeated in tones of sadness, indignation, pleading and hope. 'Special Class Prize. . . bouncy castle . . . candy floss stall . . . better than Class 4a . . . better than a bouncy castle . . .'

Miss Gilhoolie slid down her pillows so that she was lying flat and a cascade of diamonds tumbled to the floor.

'Something better than a candy floss stall is what we need,' continued Dougal as he grovelled under the bed collecting the diamonds up again and began to stuff them under her pillow. 'Scruffs and Nutters, that's what they call us . . . Summer fair and nothing for us to do . . . Balloon racing and hot dogs . . . something better than Class 4a . . .'

Dougal was a genius when it came to pestering unwilling listeners. He had seven older sisters at home on whom he had constantly practised. He could keep it up for hours.

'Summer fair,' heard Miss Gilhoolie for about the fortieth time. 'Only two days away . . . better than a bouncy castle we need . . . something exciting . . .'

'Dougal!' moaned Miss Gilhoolie. 'Go away!'

'But you haven't thought of anything yet,' said Dougal indignantly, and began again.' . . . Fair . . . bouncy castle . . . candy floss stall . . .'

'Whoever heard such rubbish?' demanded Miss Gilhoolie at one point. 'Schools don't have fairs! There is nothing in my teaching contract about organising fairs!'

'Every year!' Dougal told her patiently. 'Every year we have a fair! Everyone does something, every class I mean. This year there's going to be a Special Class Prize for the people who make the most money. Class 4a are saying they've won it already. They're having a bouncy castle and a candy floss stall and hot dogs and a balloon race . . .'

'Yes, yes, you said,' moaned Miss Gilhoolie. 'Go home now Dougal!'

'I don't think I ought to go home until you think of something,' said Dougal virtuously. 'They would be so disappointed, Simon and Madeline and Samuel and all the rest. I told you 4a are having a bouncy castle, didn't I? And a candy floss stall and . . .'

'Dougal,' interrupted Miss Gilhoolie faintly. 'I'll think of something. I will. But please go home!'

'Yes, but it will have to be good,' said Dougal. 'Because 4a have got a bouncy . . .'

'It will be good,' said Miss Gilhoolie pulling

herself up and opening her eyes and trying to look firm.

'What, better than a b . . .'

'Better than a bouncy castle, of course! And a candy floss stall and a hot dog stand and a ballon race! Better than anything you've ever seen!'

'What is it then?' asked Dougal.

'Really Dougal!' exclaimed Miss Gilhoolie, almost as if she was well again. 'Go home at once! I have told you I will think of something!'

'I only wondered . . .' began Dougal.

'I will have it sent to the school.'

'It's just because 4a . . .'

'I know, I know! Talk about something else, please Dougal!' She sounded quite pathetic and Dougal was touched.

'Sir Lancelot misses you, Madeline says.'

'Does he?'

'We all do. You won't forget, will you? About the fair I mean?'

'No, no. I'll remember the fair.'

'I'll go then, shall I?' asked Dougal.

'Yes please,' said Miss Gilhoolie.

Outside the hospital Simon Percy counted cars. He counted aeroplanes overhead. He played the name game, where you give instant imaginary names to every stranger that passes. He worked out how he would spend a million pounds if he had a million pounds. He wrote his name in a mosaic of car park pebbles, trained an ant to fetch grass seeds and worked out all the different days of the week his birthday would fall on until he was a hundred and two. After that he simply sat and stared at the hospital doors, and at last Dougal came.

Dougal was very bouncy. He might not have been noticed on his way in to visit Miss Gilhoolie, but he had certainly been noticed on his way out again. His disguise had been admired by the whole hospital. The patient he had startled into running down a corridor had told him that doctors had given up hope of her ever walking again. He had been thanked by her relations, photographed for the hospital newspaper, interviewed on hospital radio and feasted on hospital food.

'But what about Miss Gilhoolie?' asked Simon.

'She's thinking of something,' said Dougal.

'She's thinking of something,' Dougal told Class 4b. They were out in the playground before school the next morning and Dougal was trying to answer a storm of questions. 'Yes, she still smells of magic! Well, of course she was pleased to see me! Loads of flowers! I suppose she did look illish! No, not pretty at all Samantha! How could she, in bed? I didn't forget to tell her about the bouncy castle! I didn't forget anything! It's being sent to the school!'

'*What* is?' asked several people, but instead of answering, Dougal pointed.

Four huge lorries were crawling slowly up Pudding Bag Lane, three green and one black. They turned into Pudding Bag School, entirely filling the car park.

CHAPTER THREE

What Came Out of The Lorries

Total silence fell as Class 4b stared at the four enormous lorries that had just arrived.

'Stationery and catering comes in big lorries,' said Madeline at last, but she sounded very uncertain and somehow everyone knew that this was no ordinary school delivery of stationery or catering. When the engines were turned off a great deal of excited sniffing and nudging took place, and even Sir Lancelot looked slightly interested for a moment, and stopped chewing moose nuts and snuffled the air.

Just then the bell went, and Class 4b had to tear themselves away and go and line up, along with the rest of the school, outside the cloakroom doors. To their astonishment nobody else seemed in the least bit interested in the new arrivals to the school car park.

'Stop *whispering*, Class 4b!' ordered the secretary as she shepherded them in. 'Dougal dear, get in line and stop waving your arms about!'

'But . . .' began Dougal.

'*Quiet!*' said the school secretary, who was beside herself with distraction, what with Miss Gilhoolie being so ill, next year's timetable still unarranged, the Summer Fair only twenty-four hours away and the Head never properly replaced since the last one had been blasted off into space two terms earlier by Class 4b.

'Take the register please, Madeline dear,' she said when they were all sitting down. 'Then you must all choose new library books and sit and read them quietly until someone comes to sort you out. I will try to pop in from time to time but I cannot be running backwards and forwards from the office all day with all I have to do!'

'But Miss Gilhoolie usually issues our library books,' said Samantha.

'I cannot help that,' said the secretary. 'You must issue your own. Someone must come to me for the key, someone must stamp them and someone else must take the tickets . . . *Please* stop making difficulties, children dear!'

'Has Miss Gilhoolie sent us any messages today?' Samuel asked, seeing that she was already edging her way towards the classroom door. 'Because she said she would and we've just seen . . .'

'I'm afraid not, dear. Now I really *must* go!'

'She said she'd send something for the school summer fair,' said Simon. 'Didn't she, Dougal?'

Dougal, who had been quietly balanced on a radiator with his body half out of a window trying to see round corners, came back in at the sound of his name and said,

'Those four HUGE lorries are still in the car park! Three green and one . . .'

But the secretary was determined not to

waste time listening to descriptions of lorries, no matter how huge and green.

'Catering and stationery, I expect,' she said, clutching the register and backing out of the door. 'Catering and stationery, so close the window, dear!'

'And one black,' Dougal told her, climbing down. 'Three green and one black.'

But the school secretary had gone, scuttling away like a hurried hen. She didn't see, and no one saw, the little man that climbed down from the leading lorry and headed into Pudding Bag School.

He walked straight to Class 4b, exactly as if he knew the way. This was not surprising, because he did know the way, Miss Gilhoolie had told him. He walked straight into Class 4b and up to Miss Gilhoolie's desk and an astonished silence filled the room.

The little man had a face as round as a sunflower, and his hair and whiskers, which were yellow, stuck out around it exactly like a sunflower's petals. He had a pencil behind his ear and a clipboard in one hand, and he was dressed entirely in green. Even so, except for his clothes and his size (he was even smaller than Madeline although considerably fatter) he looked completely respectable. It was not his appearance that silenced Class 4b. It was his smell. He smelt exactly like a fisherman's boot cupboard when mixed with French perfume, a healthy hedgehog, pine scented snow and a fresh west wind from the sea.

'Delivery for Mr Dougal McDougal!' announced this astonishing little man. 'Delivery for Mr Dougal McDougal from Miss Gilhoolie on account of his terrible pestering at the hospital last night! That's what I was told to say! And I was told to deliver Miss Gilhoolie's contribution to the school summer fair and to get Miss Madeline Brown to sign for it, her having more in the way of common sense! And I was told to tell you Best Love to the moose and hope you are all behaving yourselves . . .'

Whatever else he had to say was lost in the happy pandemonium that followed, during

which Dougal was thumped joyfully on the back several times and Madeline was pushed forward to sign the paper held out to her. She would have done this at once if the little man had not said reprovingly, 'You must never sign anything you haven't read first, my dear! You read it now, and then you'll know what you're getting!'

Obediently Madeline began to read aloud:

Delivery Note for Contents Described Overleaf

1. CONTENTS NOT SUITABLE FOR OPERATION BY CHILDREN UNDER 36 MONTHS
2. Trouble-Free Running of Contents Fully Guaranteed.
3. Contents not to be altered, adjusted or otherwise tampered with by any person other than the deliverer of such. *OTHERWISE TROUBLE-FREE RUNNING NOT GUARANTEED AT ALL!!!*

('That is what they call the Get Out Clause,

my dear,' explained the little man to Madeline. 'And they could not have put it plainer so mind you take note!')

4. Contents to be left clean and tidy and ready for collection 48 hours after delivery. Under NO circumstances will contents be left any longer than the allotted 48 hours.

'Now if all that sounds fair enough to you,' said the little man to Madeline, 'You sign your name along those gold and silver dots . . . Very good my dear, you might have done it all your life! Well then, all there is left to do is to tell me where you want it putting!'

'But what *is* it?' demanded twenty-six voices at once.

'Contents described Overleaf,' pointed out the little man, so Madeline turned overleaf and read aloud:

One Galloping Pony Carousel (Live Action)
One Helter-Skelter (Light House Style)

'It's a fair!' shouted Dougal McDougal. 'It's a fair for the Fair!'

One set of Dodgem Cars (Sound Effect Models)

Madeline could hardly make herself heard over the racket.

One Triple Terror Spine Freezing Other World Express

'And I must say Miss Gilhoolie only mentioned the first three items to me last night,' put in the little man. 'Highly unsuitable that other, if you ask me! Needs setting up very careful if it's to run like clockwork.'

'Bags I that one!' shrieked Dougal McDougal. 'Bags I it! I said it first! Bags I! I've bagged it now! Bags I! Bags I! Spit on my hand and hope to die!'

One or two people in Class 4b looked rather disgruntled at such a complete and ruthless grabbing, and the little man seemed very startled at Dougal's enthusiasm, especially when Dougal, a moment later, asked,

'What is it?'

'Well,' said the little man, putting on a pair of little round spectacles in order to look more closely at Dougal. 'It's what you might call a Triple Terror Spine Freezing Other World Express. As you will see for yourself when it is unpacked. And if it wasn't down on the order form I would think it had been sent by mistake."

'Miss Gilhoolie never makes mistakes,' said Dougal.

'Then she must be One in a Million,' replied the little man. 'Now, as there is Nothing Like Now and Time is Time is perhaps one of you will tell me where you would like it put.'

'What about over by the moose?' suggested Madeline, and the little, astonishing-smelling man said Over By The Moose It Is. And then he was gone.

Class 4b's windows directly overlooked the distant corner of the playing field occupied by Sir Lancelot the Brave. They spent the whole day watching out of them, and gradually, behind the section roped off by the little man and three other little men exactly like him, a fair seemed to grow out of the grass. The secretary, who scuttled in to see them from time to time, refused to take any interest in the view at all. She cried,

'Children dear, don't bother me!' and never once glanced at the little green and yellow men, hurrying about like animated dandelions between their lorries and the moose. Even when other teachers asked what on earth was going on she simply clasped her head and moaned. 'Don't *mention* Summer Fairs to me!'

All day long Miss Gilhoolie's fair for The Fair was hardly noticed at all, except by the children of course. Even when it was all in place, and the ropes were down, and the lorries had driven away, only the children were really excited. The adults, hearing who had sent it, shrugged their shoulders a little and told each other that Miss Gilhoolie always

went over the top. Class 4b were disappointed to hear that they were not allowed to inspect the now carefully covered rides. The whole playing field, they were told, was out of bounds until the following afternoon. They consoled themselves by reading and re-reading the Description Of Contents to Class 4a, and Dougal McDougal reminded people many, many times, just in case they had forgotten, that he had bagged for himself the Triple Terror Spine Freezing Other World Express. He was to regret this later.

*

That night Class 4b went home feeling happier than they had for days and days. This was a great relief to their parents, who had become very tired of hearing what useless, unhelpful people they were, and how badly they compared with the enterprising fathers and mothers of Class 4a.

'You see how nice it is to manage things for yourselves,' they said, and handed out extra pocket money to appease their consciences and promised, if at all possible, to get away from work in time to catch a glimpse of the School Summer Fair. Madeline Brown's gentle, forgetful, mad professor father promised to be there, and Dougal McDougal's seventeen-year-old sister Kate said she would not miss it for worlds.

'As long as it doesn't rain,' thought Dougal as he fell asleep that night, 'Everything will be perfect!'

It did not rain. When morning school began the next day it was already feeling hot. By lunch time it had become a perfect day of blue skies and green grass, sparkling with daisies and golden with sunshine. Class 4b had divided themselves into pairs, so that everyone would have a turn at looking after the rides and plenty of time to enjoy themselves as well. Only Dougal McDougal did not join in. He said he was staying with his Triple Terror Spine Freezing Other World Express and he would not change his mind.

'Everyone else is taking turns,' pointed out Simon Percy.

'Yes, but I bagged it!'

'You could still share!'

'No I couldn't! I *bagged* it!'

'I should think it would be boring, doing just one thing.'

'Bagging is bagging,' said Dougal, who could be very stubborn. 'You know it is!'

'Oh, all right,' said Simon. 'I do wish it was one o'clock!'

The School Summer Fair would not be open to visitors until two o'clock, but from one o'clock onwards each class was to be allowed to take charge of their own particular part. This was the time when winning raffle tickets would be hidden away, bran tubs rigged, candy floss sampled and the best of the book and cake and sweet stalls reserved at extra-low prices for the stall holders themselves.

Class 4b gave not a thought to these enterprising activities. All they cared about was that at one o'clock they would be able to try out their rides. They hung about Sir Lancelot, waiting for the hour to come. When it struck at last they rushed to pull back the green canvas covers, and what they found was beyond their wildest dreams.

The Galloping Pony Carousel was the first thing to be set in motion, dappled ponies of gold and silver with red and blue and green saddles and bridles, each on a barley sugar twisted pole. In the centre was a barrel organ and two large buttons, green to go and red to stop.

'But they come alive!' shrieked Emma, one of the first to have a ride, and it was true. No sooner did the music start than golden ears began to flicker, silver manes tossed, and painted bodies grew warm and breathing. As the carousel turned faster and faster the barley sugar poles seemed to melt completely away and the ponies began a canter that became a gallop.

'They're racing!' squealed Charlotte, as she clutched her pony's mane, and so they were, racing so fast that the fairground blurred into a rainbow of light, and there was nothing to be seen except a circle of colour, and the running ponies, and nothing to be heard

except the wild, jangling music of the barrel organ and shrill neighs of delight.

When the carousel stopped it felt for a moment like the world had stopped with it. The riders slid down from their painted ponies and gazed at each other, dazzled and disbelieving, and all round them was the smell of magic.

The Lighthouse Helter Skelter was a much quieter affair altogether. There was a pile of mats at the bottom and a staircase that spiralled round and round the inside of the red and white striped tower until it reached a circular balcony at the top. In the centre was a great revolving light enclosed in a faceted globe so that a thousand glitters dazzled the eyes. There was a railed barrier enclosing the balcony and a little flat platform where you placed your mat before sitting down and whizzing round and round to the bottom of the tower. Simon Percy did not sit down straight away, but turned his back to the dazzling light and looked outwards over the railed barrier and far away, deep in the blue, he saw a sailing ship. He rubbed his eyes and looked again and dolphins were leaping. Beside him Samuel Moon said in a stunned whisper,

'Look at the waves!'

There was seascape after seascape, they changed as Simon moved around the balcony, desert islands and flying fish, pounding waves and rocky headlands. They lasted until he inadvertently stepped onto somebody's mat on the starting platform, and found himself shooting down the slide. He would have climbed straight back up for another go at once if Madeline had not grabbed him and shouted.

'Come and look at the dodgems!'

The dodgems were a whirl of colour. There were old-fashioned fire engines with large brass bells, ice cream vans playing ice cream music, traction engines that blew out steam with ear splitting whistles, a double decker bus that you drove from upstairs and a miniature Silver Ghost Rolls-Royce that purred like a cat. Also there was a bright red

Ferrari, a yellow combine harvester, a safari Jeep and a long, low, pale pink saloon. They did not crash, but bounced from each other as if held apart by invisible force fields, and they went very fast. As they turned and cornered great spurts of coloured stars shot from their wheels.

Dougal McDougal was saving the best till last. He had ridden on a silver dappled pony, slid twice down the Helter Skelter, and done handbrake turns on a combine harvester in a cloud of green sparks. His expectations could not possibly have been higher as he ran to pull the covers off the Triple Terror Spine Freezing Other World Express.

CHAPTER FOUR

What Happened in The Afternoon

The Triple Terror Spine Freezing Other World Express was the only ride still covered up.

'I'll uncover it myself,' Dougal had said when Simon and Samuel had kindly offered to help. 'I bagged it!'

The covers were much shabbier and dirtier than the ones that had been over the other rides. Dougal began pulling them away and the first thing to appear was a blackboard.

In twirly curly writing it gave a description of what was in store for anyone who was planning to take a ride. It read:

Pass Through the Icy Cavern
Vanish Utterly Into The Dark
Explore Dramatic Dragon Land
and finally
APPEAR FOR YOUR FREE COLOUR
PHOTOGRAPH UNDER THE BLAZE OF
THE NORTHERN LIGHTS!

Oh, thought Dougal, and something deep inside him gave a very small twinge of disappointment, because it wasn't quite what he had expected of a Triple Terror Spine Freezing Other World Express. He felt slightly worried as he tugged away the rest of the covers.

Underneath was a round raised platform with steps up one side and the green grass of the playing field showing clearly underneath. It was obviously put together in sections like the slices of a cake. Around the platform ran a little circular track, two thirds of it hidden under a dirty, black wooden tunnel. On the part that was out in the open there stood a shabby little train, four small open carriages strung together behind a battered looking engine. Beside the entrance of the tunnel were two buttons, a green one labelled 'GO' and a red one labelled 'STOP'. There was a mustiness in the air that came from old canvas and rust and damp wood, but not a trace of the smell of magic that lingered round the carousel, or was carried in the breeze that blew on the top of the lighthouse, or arose from the clouds of coloured stars that streamed behind the dodgems.

Dougal stared at all this, the little track and the train and the dingy wooden tunnel, and he was completely baffled. All the same, he did not entirely give up hope. He climbed aboard, and reached out and pressed the green button.

'The surprise must be inside,' he told himself firmly as the engine clanked to a start.

There were swing doors at each end of the tunnel. The entrance ones creaked open as the engine pushed into them, and Dougal was inside.

'I suppose this is the Icy Cavern,' he thought

rather dismally as he looked around.

The Icy Cavern was short and blue. There was a slight draught and plastic icicles. Dougal's spine was certainly chilled, but with disappointment rather than cold.

The Icy Cavern ended with a thick black curtain that parted in front of the train. This, it seemed, was where Dougal was supposed to vanish utterly into the dark. Dramatic Dragon Land followed immediately, and here the train came to a stop so that passengers could admire the luminous paintings of cartoon dragons on the inside of the tunnel walls. Dougal looked at them with deep contempt and while he was looking the Northern Lights came on: pink and blue light bulbs strung across the roof. At this point there was a loud click, the train chugged back into daylight again and a small and sticky photograph was delivered from a slot in the cab. It showed the train with its solitary passenger, staring dismally up at the light bulbs.

The little green and yellow men had gone to some trouble to set it up to run like clockwork, and run like clockwork it did. There was nothing magicky about it at all.

Dougal could not believe his bad luck. He climbed back into the train and went round again, and then again and again. With each trip the train seemed slower, the icy cavern warmer, the black out curtain more tatty and worn, the dragons less dragony, and the Northern Lights more light bulby. Each Free Colour Photograph showed an expression of increasing gloom.

After the fourth trip Dougal was joined by a group of people from Class 4b and they forced him to give them a ride.

'Oh, all right,' said Dougal reluctantly, 'but you won't like it!'

'It doesn't look all that scary,' remarked Samantha.

'The magic's probably inside,' said Madeline wisely. 'Isn't it Dougal?'

Dougal turned his back and pretended not to hear.

'Come round with us,' urged Samuel.

'No thanks,' said Dougal, not looking round.

'Is there something wrong?'

'You'll see in a minute,' said Dougal, and pressed the green button.

Three minutes later everyone completely understood.

'Poor old Dougal,' said Samuel. 'What an awful swizz!'

'We'll take turns,' said Madeline. 'You don't have to stay with it just because you bagged it!'

'Let's just put the covers back and forget about it,' suggested Samantha. 'Nobody's going to want to ride on a thing like that!'

Dougal, who didn't like being called 'poor old Dougal', said nobody had asked for Samantha's opinion, that it was a perfectly good ride and he wasn't going to cover it up, and that he had bagged it and would stay with it for as long as he wanted. Then he went and fiddled with his blackboard and ignored them all. And when they still persisted in hanging round looking sorry for him he suggested very rudely that they should all buzz off.

As the afternoon went on the fair grew more and more busy. There were queues for everything except the Triple Terror Express. Its only customers were a few sticky two and three year olds, dumped by their relations for three minutes peace. The photographs of their faces showed expressions of complete boredom.

'They didn't like it,' said their mothers, when Dougal demanded his pay. 'You can see they didn't like it! Anyway, what about Under Threes Going Free?'

'I never said that!' said Dougal, outraged.

'Well you ought!' said the toddlers' mothers. 'A big boy like you!'

'Kids!' muttered Dougal in disgust, and took to disappearing around the back of the ride whenever a new set appeared.

It was while he was skulking at the back of the tunnel that he noticed the labels. They were painted on the sides of each section of the platform. Each had a number and a brief description.

1 (*Icy Cavern*) 4 (*Vanish*) 2 (*Dragons*)
3 (*Northern Lights*)

Those were the parts that were under the tunnel.

5 (*Uncovered*) 6 (*Uncovered*)

Those were the parts in the light.

'That's funny,' said Dougal, and went round them again. 'One,' he read. 'Four, two three, and then five and six, that's when you come out again.'

He drew a plan on his hand with a Biro of the platform and the numbers.

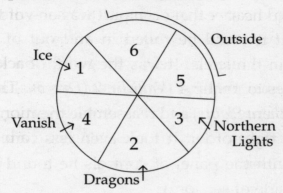

And then he drew how he thought it should be.

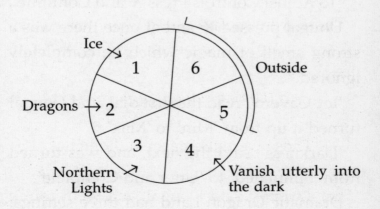

'It's been put together wrong,' he thought crossly, and began inspecting the fastenings that held each section to the next. They were bolts, and they sprang open at Dougal's first tug, and he saw that each part was on wheels so that it could be rolled in and out of its place in the circle. It was the work of a few minutes to unclip 4 (*Vanish*), 2 (*Dragons*) and 3 (*Northern Lights*) and reassemble them again in the right order. It took even less time to deal with the panel of controls he found on the inside of section 1.

'NO UNAUTHORISED ACCESS' it said at the top, and then

'To Adjust Controls Press ✱ and Continue'.

Dougal pressed ✱ and at once there was a strong smell of magic which he completely ignored.

'Icy Cavern', read the first dial, and Dougal turned it up from 'Min' to 'Max'.

'Darkness', said the next, and was turned from 'Simulated' to 'Utter and Complete'.

Dramatic Dragon Land had three settings: 'Illustrated', 'Animated', and 'Live'.

Dougal unhesitatingly turned it from 'Illustrated' to 'Live'.

Northern Lights he switched from 'Back Up' to 'Main'.

'Now all I have to change is the notice board!' he said, and rubbed out the twirly curly writing and wrote instead in his own plain scrawl the new order of events, as rearranged by Dougal McDougal.

Pass Through The Icy Cavern
Explore Dramatic Dragon Land
Appear for your Free Colour Photograph
Under the Blaze of the
Northern Lights
and finally
Vanish Utterly Into The Dark!

'There!' said Dougal, wiping his chalky hands on the front of his shirt and looking quite affectionately at his shabby little train. He was about to climb aboard and check the improvements for himself when six school governors turned up altogether and insisted, with much joking, on being given a ride. They entirely filled the little carriages, laden as they were with produce from every stall, but with many exclamations and much loud laughter they packed themselves in and announced they were ready to start.

'But what about paying?' asked Dougal, who so far had not earned a single penny, having not charged himself and his friends, quite apart from the cheating behaviour of the toddlers' mothers. 'What about paying? Fifty pence each!'

The governers laughed heartily and said he was a fine business man.

'A credit to your school!' said one. 'But we're wedged in so tight we can't get to our pockets.'

'Oh well,' said Dougal slightly grumpily. 'As long as you give it to me when you get out.'

This caused even more irritating laughter.

'Grown ups!' thought Dougal scornfully, and pressed the green button and watched as the train, creaking terribly with the weight of

so many governors to pull, chugged slowly through the tunnel entrance and out of sight. Loud shrieks came from under the little wooden cover of the Triple Terror Express, followed by a most complete and absolute silence.

'Dougal! Dougal!' called an excited voice at that moment, and Dougal looked up and saw Simon Percy waving to him from the top of the Helter Skelter. 'Dougal, come quick! We've spotted a whale!'

A whale was impossible to resist, and Dougal was tired of sulking. He abandoned the governors without another thought and dashed across to join his friends. They were all exclaiming and pointing with delight at a new view that had just appeared, whales leaping in among the icefloes of a distant arctic sea.

'It's when you're looking straight outwards that you see things,' explained Simon to Dougal. 'It's like they were in the sky except of course they're not. Those whales are in a real sea! If you listen really hard you can hear the splashes, and the cracking creaking sounds must be the ice! But if you look straight down it's just playing field! It feels really weird!'

He looked down as he spoke, and then suddenly exclaimed,

'Hey Dougal! Your train's going round and round with no one in it!'

'So it is,' said Dougal, looking down as well. 'I started it off with a whole load of governors inside but then I came up here. I forgot about stopping it.'

'They must have got sick of going round and round and jumped off!' said Simon.

'What a cheek!' exclaimed Dougal, 'And they hadn't paid! OY!'

Three big boys were running towards Dougal's train, obviously having seen that it was unattended and being intent of a free ride. They looked up at Dougal and laughed and leapt on board.

'I'm going to get them!' said Dougal, seizing the mat he had carried up with him and flinging himself down the slide. 'It's fifty pence a go! Oh!'

He shot off the end of the Helter Skelter just in time to see the train re-emerge. It was completely empty.

'They must have seen you coming after them and escaped through the back,' said Simon, puffing up to join him. 'What a lovely smell! Can I have a go now?'

The smell of Dougal's train was now most definitely magical.

'I mended it,' he said proudly. 'Let's both have a go. Oh no! Look what's coming! Let's not!'

Two exhausted-looking mothers were approaching, each pushing empty double buggies. Behind them followed five grizzling toddlers.

'Want to go wound and wound!' bawled one of them, and wiped its nose on its mother's sleeve.

'We just need somewhere to leave them for a few minutes,' one of the mothers told Dougal as Simon scrambled hastily out and tried to look as if he had never thought of going anywhere. 'Someone told us this

70

was a nice quiet ride.'

'Want to go wound and wound!'

'I suppose they *can* go round and round?' asked the other mother.

'If you pay for each time they can,' said Dougal, determined to get some money at last. 'Fifty pence a time. Each. It takes about three minutes. Two pounds fifty a time it will be if they all go.'

'Isn't there a discount if they have more than one ride?'

'No,' said Dougal firmly and stepped hastily backwards as the toddler with the streaming nose lunged towards him. 'No, there isn't.'

'Want to go *wound and wound!*'

'You shall go round and round,' said the wailer's mother dumping it in a carriage with a groan of exasperation. 'Come on! Let's load them all in and have a few minutes peace!'

'How many times round?' asked Dougal. 'Ten times would take half an hour. What about that?'

'How much would it be?'

'Twenty five pounds,' said Dougal unblushingly, and held out his hand.

'Twenty five pounds!' the mothers shrieked. 'That is utterly ridiculous! . . . Oh very well!'

The wails from the carriages, which had become quite deafening, suddenly switched off, five five pound notes were counted into Dougal's palm and the green button was pressed. Eager to make the most of their investment the two mothers disappeared into the crowd without a second glance, and Dougal, with the Triple Terror Express taken care of for the next half hour, rushed back to the Helter Skelter. The whales had gone and been replaced by sea lions, and after that there was a giant squid, followed by a tropical storm. Then the wild music of the carousel tempted Dougal back down the Helter Skelter and onto a bucking silver pony, and from there he went to the dodgems, where he managed to grab the Ferrari and shot off in a cloud of crimson sparks.

It was much, much later, as he wandered

contentedly back from the candy floss stall, that Dougal was reminded of his customers on the Triple Terror Express. He might not have remembered them for even longer had he not been suddenly pounced on from behind.

It was his customers' mothers. They seized him and shook him and marched him back to his train.

'You naughty, naughty boy!' they exclaimed as they propelled him along. 'What do you mean by leaving them? Why didn't you stay with them? What do you think you've been doing all this time? We looked for you everywhere! Why did you let them go and *where have they gone? Look*!'

The toddlers' mothers, having now reached the Triple Terror Other World Spine Freezing Express, pointed furiously to the little train, still trundling slowly round its track, but now completely empty.

'Oh,' said Dougal.

'Don't just stand there saying Oh! What have you done with them?'

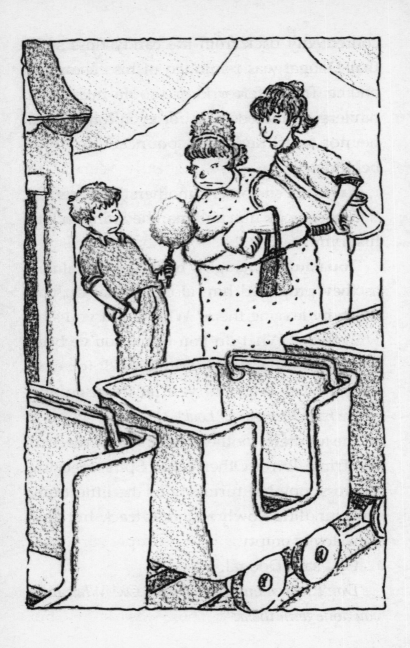

'I haven't done anything with them,' said Dougal indignantly. 'I just started them off and came away. Round and round, you said, while you had a bit of peace! I *thought* you wanted to get rid of them!'

This tactless reminder only seemed to infuriate the two mothers more than ever.

'Do you mean to tell us,' they demanded, 'that you don't know what's happened?'

Dougal took a large bite of candyfloss and the whole bundle came off its stick and glued itself onto his chin.

'P'raps they fell out,' he suggested, carefully scraping off his new pink and yellow beard with his candyfloss stick and eating the shavings between scrapes. 'You know, in the tunnel. And they've gone to sleep, or something . . .'

'Gone to sleep!' repeated the mothers. 'Fell out!' And without another word they pushed past Dougal and jumped onto the train.

'But you haven't paid!' protested Dougal.

There was no reply. There was a shriek, but

whether of Triple Terror or simple indignation Dougal could not tell. Three minutes later, the train reappeared, completely empty.

'That's very funny,' said Dougal McDougal.

CHAPTER FIVE
A Bit At A Time

Madeline Brown was a very intelligent child. She noticed things and thought about them. She realised, for instance, that although there are some things it is possible to believe in all in one go, there are other things (many more things) that is only possible to believe in a bit at a time.

'Miss Gilhoolie's Fair is a bit-at-a-time thing,' she remarked.

'What?' said Samantha.

'Nothing,' said Madeline, who never had much luck when she tried explaining her thoughts to Samantha.

'You don't want to start going bonkers like your dad,' warned Samantha kindly.

'No,' agreed Madeline, but all the same she thought Miss Gilhoolie's fair was a bit-at-a-time thing. The magical ponies, the distant views from the top of the lighthouse, the sparkling splendour of the dodgems, had all seemed too good to be true in the beginning. It was only after several turns of each that people began to expect that the ponies would really canter, that magic seas would actually be visible, and that each dodgem would truly skim away with its own comet tail of coloured stars.

The same sort of thing was happening with Dougal and the Triple Terror Express. He could not bring himself to believe that people were actually vanishing.

The school secretary was the next to go. In the short time that she had known Dougal she had become quite fond of him. It was a shame, she thought, that he should have been left in charge of such a shabby little ride. She pretended to be extra-enthusiastic, just because it was so shabby, and told him, as she handed over her money, that she had purposely saved the best till last.

'I think the dodgems are the best,' said Dougal, looking at the fifty pence piece she had given him as if he wished it would go away.

'Oh, no, no, no, no, no!' said the secretary. 'Much too noisy!'

'Well, the Helter Skelter then.'

'Much, much, much, much, much too high!'

'You ought to try the roundabout though!'

'Far, far, far, far, far too fast for me! Is anything wrong, Dougal dear?'

'Oh, no,' said Dougal, almost completely certain that people did not just disappear into thin air.

'Then off we go!' said the school secretary.

Dougal put her money in his pocket and helped her aboard with the strangest feeling of doubt.

'I shall hold on tight!' she called, waving cheerily to him.

'It *can't* be true,' said Dougal, and pressed the green button.

Three minutes later the empty train

reappeared. Even then Dougal could not believe what was happening. He tested it again, this time with the reception class teacher and the school nurse. They also disappeared.

Then, for a moment, Dougal allowed himself to know that it was true, and that the Triple Terror Express no longer ran like boring clockwork, but ran like highly dangerous magic instead.

'No, no, no!' he said madly, and in a desperate attempt to prove himself wrong grew completely reckless and chalked up a new notice on his board which read,

ALL RIDES ½ PRICE

In this way he eliminated two large families, four teachers and several unaccompanied children, without hardly pausing for thought. Still he was not convinced.

He took to starting people off and then dashing round the back in the hope of finding them escaping under the canvas. They never did. He lost six school cleaners and the lollipop lady while, with his ear pressed to the tunnel wall, he listened for voices that never came. He remembered the photographs and hurried round to the engine to see if there was any clue to be had from there. It made grinding, whirring noises but appeared to have jammed. He groaned with despair and beat at it with his two fists and he was still doing this when his sister Kate arrived.

'What's up Dougal darling?' she asked cheerfully. 'Has something gone wrong?'

'Dougal stopped his hammering, sank wearily down onto the platform steps, and buried his head in his hands.

'Dougal *darling*!' exclaimed Kate, in alarm, having never before seen Dougal quite so lacking in bounce. 'Dougal, whatever is the matter?'

'My train keeps disappearing people,' said Dougal, admitting it at last.

'Your train keeps *what*?'

'Disappearing people. They get on, and I

start them off, and they disappear!'

'Gosh!' said Kate. 'How really useful! I know a lot of people I'd like to put on your train!'

'It isn't funny!' cried Dougal in anguish.

'Dougal darling, don't be silly! I expect they crawl off half way round.'

'They don't.'

'To trick you.'

'It isn't like that.' Dougal's head sank lower and lower and Kate stared at him in dismay.

'They wouldn't mean to upset you. Just as a joke.'

'You don't understand,' said Dougal.

'I'll tell you what! I'll have a go! I promise not to disappear!'

'No!'

Startled into action Dougal leapt to his feet, but not before Kate had pressed the green button and climbed nimbly aboard. He flung himself onto the red STOP button, but it was too late.

Then Dougal felt very bad. Worse than he had felt when he had chopped up his teacher's desk to make a sledge. Worse than when he had discovered he had eaten the school gerbils by mistake. Worse, even, than when he had accidently blasted his good friend Madeline Brown into deepest space. Quite numb with shock he vanished the whole of class 2a in three packed trainloads-full without hardly noticing they had gone.

He was dismally polishing the engine with his handful of five pound notes when Madeline Brown arrived.

'There's ever such a strong smell of magic around here,' she remarked at once.

'Is there?' asked Dougal gloomily.

'Haven't you noticed? What's the matter?'

'I've lost Kate.'

'How?'

Dougal demonstrated how with two passing remedial teachers.

'Dougal! Have you lost any more?'

'Dozens!'

'Oh, Dougal!'

Sir Lancelot the Brave, completely bored with

summer fairs, had spent the afternoon patiently gnawing through his tether. He looked up from his triumphant last bite to see his favourite slave, Madeline Brown, standing only a little distance away. A vision of moose nuts filled his mind and he began a lumbering gallop.

He was thinking only of food as he galloped straight across the platform of the Triple Terror Express. He did not intend to catch the green 'GO' button with his antler, but he did. He did not notice that the little engine had started, but it had. He certainly did not mean to go for a ride, but the last of the little carriages caught him neatly between his legs, and he was whisked away. It crossed his mind as he shot backwards into the tunnel that this was not the usual way of getting moose nuts at all.

'Lancelot!' shrieked Madeline in dismay, and then there was a loud bellow and a grinding crunch and the Triple Terror Express stopped, the tail end of its last carriage just sticking out of the entrance tunnel. Sir

Lancelot had been too much for it, and the mechanism had jammed.

Dougal and Madeline seized the last carriage and pulled and pulled.

The smell of magic was now so strong that it made them quite giddy. So did the icy coldness of the air that came out of the tunnel.

'I think the wheels must be frozen!' gasped Dougal.

'Try once more!' said Madeline, through chattering teeth. 'One, two, three!'

At 'Three' they flung themselves backwards with all their weight and in the tunnel something gave way. Gradually the train reappeared, and with it came Sir Lancelot, only a changed Sir Lancelot. His coat was so heavy with frost that he sparkled as if he was covered in thick white glittering fur. Icicles hung from his antlers. He looked very, very alarmed, and this for an animal who had never shown any emotion except greed, was most surprising of all.

Dougal touched his fur and remembered the Icy Cavern dial that he had deliberately turned from 'Min' to 'Max', and felt quite sick.

The struggle to rescue Sir Lancelot seemed to have unjammed something in the mechanism of the train, because the slot in the front of the engine began suddenly to churn out photographs. They fell in sticky strips to the floor, dozens of them, tangled together in bunches. Madeline and Dougal tore themselves away from the sight of the already rapidly thawing Sir Lancelot to gather them up. Many of them were stuck face to face, or torn and twisted, but among them were plenty that were still clear. They showed Dougal and Madeline the fate of the disappeared.

'Here's Kate,' said Dougal, faint with thankfulness, and there was Kate, with frosted hair and startled eyes, under the blaze of a sky full of rainbows.

'The Northern Lights?' wondered Madeline, and Dougal remembered the control that he had turned from 'Back Up' to 'Main'.

Kate appeared to be negotiating with a dragon.

'A real live dragon!' said Madeline wonderingly.

'Yes,' said Dougal.

The Midsummer sunshine was as hot as ever, but the afternoon was coming to an end at last. The crowds were quickly thinning, there were no longer queues for the rides, and people were beginning to appear with black bin bags and pointed sticks, collecting rubbish. Sir Lancelot, now thawed and comforted with moosenuts, stood steaming in the sunshine.

'What I can't understand,' said Madeline, as she turned and turned the photographs, 'Is why it suddenly started to happen. It was perfectly all right at first. Not magicky at all.'

'It was put together wrong,' said Dougal.

'It was what?'

'Put together wrong. I fixed it.'

Madeline stared at him, open mouthed. Dougal swallowed but bravely carried on.

'It was so boring. You know it was. And everyone was being sorry for me. I can't bear people being sorry for me. I took it to bits.'

'You took it to bits???'

'And rearranged it.'

Madeline began to search feverishly through her pockets. She found what she was looking for, the delivery note that had been left with her the day before. She held it out to Dougal, pointing with a finger that trembled a little to Condition Number 3.

3. Contents not to be altered, adjusted or otherwise tampered with by any person other that the deliverer of such. *OTHERWISE TROUBLE*

*FREE RUNNING NOT GUARANTEED AT
ALL!!!*

'Well, I forgot,' said Dougal.

'Oh Dougal!'

'I hate it when people say "Oh Dougal"! I turned up the controls as well.'

'Oh . . .'

'Icy Cavern from "Min" to "Max". Darkness from "Simulated" to "Utter and Complete". The dragons from "Illustrated" to "Live" and the Northern Lights from "Back Up" to "Main". And I changed the blackboard too, to show what happens now!'

Madeline looked at the blackboard, where the little green man's twirly curly writing had been, and read the new version aloud.

'Pass Through The Icy Cavern
Explore Dramatic Dragon Land
Appear for your Photograph under the
Blaze of the Northern Lights
and finally
Disappear Utterly Into the Dark

'Oh Dougal!' said Madeline.

'You said it again!' said Dougal crossly. 'You might do something to help, instead of just 'Oh Dougal'-ing me! I've been trying to get it back to how it was before I changed it. I've tried and tried, but I can't on my own. It's stuck!'

Madeline jumped to her feet, ashamed of not having thought of this obvious solution herself.

'It's made in sections,' said Dougal, following her round to the back of the ride. 'They unclip and move on wheels and you can swop them round. They went together really easily. Just like a jigsaw when you get the pieces right, but look at them now! Nothing could be stucker!'

This was true. Madeline and Dougal hammered and prized and thumped until their hands were sore and throbbing. They succeeded in opening a small chink between sections 2 and 3 (Explore Dramatic Dragon Land and Appear For Your Photograph Under

The Blaze Of The Northern Lights) but that was all.

'In the morning,' said Dougal, sinking back into despair. 'The little men will come and take it away. And everyone in it. Kate. All of them.'

'Perhaps the little men will be able to get them out.'

'What's left of them you mean,' said Dougal, even more gloomily. 'After the dragons and the cold all night.'

'Oh Doug . . .' began Madeline again, but was interrupted.

'What's the matter?'

It was Simon Percy. He had just arrived with Samuel Moon and Charlotte and Emma the twins.

'You'd better tell them,' said Madeline, and once again Dougal recited the story of his rearranging of the Triple Terror Express. He was demonstrating the complete stuckness of the sections when a voice from behind remarked, 'Probably frozen.'

'Father!' cried Madeline, and everyone

turned to see Professor Brown, Madeline's vague but kindly father, gazing thoughtfully down at them.

'Having overheard your conversation,' said Professor Brown politely, 'and observed the condition of the moose, I should infer that the parts are probably not so much stuck as frozen. As for the Vanishing Trick . . .'

Nobody heard what Madeline's father thought about the Vanishing Trick because at that moment there was a sound from the Triple Terror Express. A squeal of alarm, and then several more squeals, and then before the astonished eyes of Dougal and his friends, a shape appeared. It slid out of the little crack between sections 2 and 3 that Madeline and Dougal had managed to open.

It came out flat, like a person-shaped double-sided photograph, but as it emerged it rounded out, exactly like a flat balloon rounds out when it is blown up. By the time it had landed onto the grass it was completely itself once more.

'Oh, oh!' shrieked Dougal, seizing it in his

arms as if it might vanish again at any moment. 'It's one of my babies! It's the one with the runny nose!'

The toddler was followed by another, and then another, and finally two more, tangled together in a muddle of arms and legs.

'My babies, my babies!' cried Dougal, gathering them up as if they were money. 'Are they all right?'

'They look all right,' said Charlotte, as she and Emma began cautiously untangling them. 'Mucky of course . . .'

'They *were* mucky,' interrupted Dougal excitedly, still clutching his toddler to his chest. 'This one especially!'

'. . . and very cold . . .'

'Put them into the sun,' said Madeline, bending to help Charlotte and Emma. 'Give me that one Dougal!'

But the toddler pulled itself out of Dougal's arms, curled up in a patch of sunshine, stuck its thumb in its mouth, and closed its eyes.

'It's the one that wanted to go round and round,' said Dougal, hanging lovingly over it.

'But how did they get here?' wondered Madeline.

The toddler opened his eyes and unplugged his thumb for a few moments.

'Fell down a cwack,' he said.

'Just as I thought,' said Madeline's father, sitting down beside the sleeping children and resting his chin comfortably on his bony knees. 'True vanishment would be impossible of course, but a temporary loss of dimensions . . .'

'They came out flat,' interrupted Madeline, trying to explain it to herself.

'Two dimensional,' agreed her father.

'Up and across, like a picture.'

'Exactly.'

'But they've rounded out now.'

'They've regained their third dimensions. Should they have *lost* another dimension instead . . .'

'They'd be straight lines,' said Madeline. 'Up and down or across, but not both.'

'Quite so.'

'And a dimension less than that would be a dot.'

'An invisible dot,' corrected Professor Brown.

'That's when they vanish utterly.'

Professor Brown said that there was a world of difference between being an invisible dot and vanishing utterly, and Dougal, who had been listening to this scholarly discussion with more and more impatience, drew Simon and Samuel aside.

'I'm going inside,' he told them quietly. 'I've

got to find Kate. If those kids were all right, then I'll be all right too . . .'

'I'll come with you,' interrupted Simon at once, and Samuel, although much less eagerly, nodded to say that he would come as well.

'But someone's got to stay behind and get rid of anyone who starts making problems,' said Dougal. 'I thought you two would help Madeline with that.'

'It won't take both of us,' said Simon. 'Sam could stay, couldn't you Sam? Do you mind?'

Samuel, much relieved, said he didn't mind at all.

'You don't have to come Simon,' said Dougal.

'I've never seen dragons.'

'All right then.'

Behind the Triple Terror Express the toddlers slept in the late afternoon sunshine, guarded by Charlotte and Emma. Professor Brown also dozed, worn out with the impossibility of explaining the enormous difference between becoming an Invisible Dot and Vanishing

Utterly, to people who would not listen. When Madeline went round to the front of the train she found Dougal and Simon were already gone, and Samuel was faithfully fulfilling his task of getting rid of questioners by co-ercing them onto the train and trundling them into nothingness. They were mostly stray teachers and the distraught parents of missing children. Everyone else had gone home.

CHAPTER SIX

Dragons and Ice

'I suppose,' said Simon, as he and Dougal climbed aboard the Triple Terror Spine Freezing Other World Express, 'this tunnel is one of those places that is bigger on the inside than the outside.'

Dougal gave his friend a very startled glance, because of course Simon must be right, and yet this thought had not occurred to him all afternoon.

'I suppose it must be,' he agreed, and his hand trembled a little as he pressed the button marked 'GO'.

'Or else,' continued Simon, talking very quickly in order to keep calm because the train had started to move, 'How would all those people you've disappeared be able to fit in. It must be *much* bigger . . . WOW!'

Simon had just seen what was inside. It was not a tunnel, it was a landscape. A blue shadowy world of ice. Ice pillars and ice mountains rose all about them. Icy winds blew. Icy distances stretched into dim icy mists in every direction. Ahead the rails shone silver, a great curve of track along which the train was travelling at incredible speed. There was no one to be seen.

'Crikey!' said Dougal.

The train ran faster and faster, speeding across the ice and the cold began to freeze them to the bone. In front they could see a long black line, stretching from left to right horizon. 'Th . . . th . . . that must be the j . . . j . . . join,' said Dougal through chattering teeth. 'I w . . . w . . . wonder . . .'

There was an enormous jolt, the line flashed black as a river of ice beneath the tracks of the train, their speed dropped dramatically, and the world turned gold.

It was the gleaming gold of sunlight

reflected on ice, but it was not sunlight. It was dragon fire. It came from the jaws of three large green dragons.

Dougal's brain skittered from one amazed thought to another as the train, now travelling quite slowly, grew closer and closer. They're as big as crocodiles! No, elephants! Longer than elephants! Were dinosaurs as big as that?

'They're the size of buses!' whispered Simon.

The dragons the size of buses were acting very strangely, leaping and squirming and lashing their tails. A small figure moved among them. It stooped and rolled something across the ice and the dragons skidded away in pursuit.

'Kate!' cried Dougal, and Kate it was, waving excitedly to the train.

'Dougal darling!' cried Kate, running beside them to keep up. 'And Simon! Simon, how nice of you to come! Do stop Dougal, I need to talk to you!'

'I don't know how!'

'With the brake!' puffed Kate. 'Oh, here they

come, back already! They *will* jump up, but it doesn't mean anything! Brake, Dougal!'

'There isn't a brake . . .' protested Dougal and then found that there was. The train ground to a halt just as the three dragons came racing up to Kate.

'Sit!' cried Kate. 'It's all right Simon, they only want to play! Good dragons! Clever dragons! Puff upwards though darlings or else it's so scorchy! Drop it then, Jelly!'

The largest dragon dropped something small and black at Kate's feet.

'We'll just leave it to cool a minute,' said Kate, touching it with her toe. 'It's a coconut I won earlier. It's been so useful . . . and they can balance it on their noses too, but it starts to smoke if they do it for long . . . Say hello to the boys then, good dragons! I gave them names . . . Jelly . . . Trifle . . . Angel Delight . . . There! It's cool enough! Off you go darlings!'

In spite of everything Dougal and Simon couldn't help smiling and Kate saw and became very severe.

'It really isn't funny!' she told them. 'You

don't know half of it yet! This weather is frightful and nobody's dressed for it. The dragons hardly take off the chill! And there have been people arriving and disappearing all afternoon, terribly over-exciting for them, you can't imagine what a nuisance they've been!'

'The people?'

'The dragons, silly!'

'They're safe *really*, aren't they?' asked Simon anxiously. 'The dragons, I mean.'

'Safe!' repeated Kate. 'Of course they're not safe! They're *dragons*, Simon darling! And they are not the only danger. A few minutes ago a whole lot of little children tumbled down a crack in the ice. Their mothers are in a terrible state, they keep vanishing and coming back flat . . . If I hadn't won that coconut I don't know what I'd do! Here they are again, you see! No peace! Lie down, good dragons! That's right, dragons have a nice sleep! Dragons go bye-byes!'

'What do you mean, coming back flat?' asked Simon, while Dougal said, 'But I can't see anybody except us.'

'You wait,' said Kate, scrambling aboard the train behind the boys. 'I'll show you what's happened to all those poor people you've been sending through! Come on! Start up Dougal!'

'But I don't know how . . .'

'Take the brake off!' said Kate impatiently. 'Dragons! Wait! *Wait*! They're worse than puppies! They take absolutely no notice! Now Dougal, stop when I tell you! Here now! Look!'

They had stopped on the near side of an another endless black line, very like the one that had caused the enormous jolt as they came up to the dragons. On the far side was a distant group of people. One of them shook a fist at Dougal.

'You can't blame her!' said Kate, and she pointed to the right, where an opening in the black line made a narrow gap in the ice that seemed to drop to bottomless blue depths.

'Those poor little children! One squeal and they were gone . . .'

'They fell down there?' asked Simon, staring.

'Yes. Look, you can see where their poor little fingers scrabbled at the edge . . .'

'But they're quite all right,' interrupted Dougal excitedly. 'They fell out onto the grass, not hurt at all. They're asleep and Charlotte and Emma are looking after them.'

'Oh thank goodness!' exclaimed Kate. 'Oh, *Sit down dragons*! They really haven't enough to do, that's the trouble! Oh, I am glad about those children! Their mothers will be so pleased if they ever find out! I wish they'd come a bit nearer so I could shout . . . *Sit down dragons*! No wonder people are frightened of you! I shan't throw it again until you are all quiet! They did come right up to the crack once, the mothers I mean, but then stupid Jelly woofed . . .'

'Can't we go and tell them?'

'Easier said than done,' Kate replied. 'Over that next black line you go flat.'

'Go flat?'

'Yes, and then you can't say a word and it

feels really odd. Like being a ghost (only I never have been), and behind *that* line, well, you can see!'

Dougal and Simon peered into the distance and saw there was another black line behind the group of soundless people. Beyond it thronged dozens of coloured straight lines.

'They look like exclamation marks!' said Simon.

'So they do,' said Kate. 'I was wondering what they reminded me of. The dots on the bottom are probably their feet. And after them, but you can't see from here, is The End, and that's the most queer of all. You go ping, like the dot in the middle of a switched off telly, and you float. You float right out of the train. You can see it go back into the open but you can't go with it. And it's dark . . .'

'Have you *been*?' demanded Dougal and Simon together.

'Oh yes!'

'Right to a dot? How did you get back?'

'I whizzed,' said Kate. 'It's as easy as anything. You can go really fast as a dot, but it's a terrible gone-away sort of feeling. And those exclamation mark things are nearly as bad. Flat's a bit better, and you sort of sail. Or you can stick with the dragons, but no one has so far, except us. And I can't think how to get out. I suppose we could try walking back through the icy waste but it would take days and days and days, even if we could manage it. And of course it's no good for anyone else, because they daren't come past the dragons . . . perhaps they would if only they'd go to sleep . . .'

'They don't look very tired,' said Simon.

'I know. All this coconut retrieving hasn't worn them out at all. I thought it might at first . . . Here we go again! Drop it then, Trifle darling! Are you *sure* those children were all right?'

'Quite,' said Dougal. 'You know Kate, those black lines that the track keeps crossing over, they must be the joins.'

'You've lost me already,' said Kate, fending off Angel Delight who was blowing like a bus-sized hairdryer in her face.

'The joins in the platform of the Triple Terror Express,' explained Dougal. 'And that crack must be where me and Madeline managed to get the sections a little bit apart.'

'You should have thought how dangerous it might be,' said Kate severely.

'And each segment leads you on a bit further to the vanishing,' continued Dougal, ignoring her. 'You go down to two dimensions in the one after the dragons, that's *why* everyone looks so flat. And then one dimension in the next section, and you look like an exclamation mark, and then no dimensions at the end. That's when you're an invisible dot. And what's after that, Kate?'

'It goes Utterly Dark,' said Kate.

'Gosh!' said Dougal, and he peered into the distance, at the flat people and the exclamation mark people and the darkness beyond, presumably alive with invisible dots. All the time there was change, as people ventured forward into more and more dimensions, and then hurriedly retreated at the closeness of the dragons. It seemed to Dougal that the least he could do, bearing in mind the fact that it was all his fault, was to have a turn at vanishing too.

'Dougal, I wish you wouldn't!' said Kate. 'I can't come with you. The dragons simply howled when I last tried to leave them, and the other passengers were so frightened they vanished into dots and didn't come back for ages.'

'I'll go with him,' said Simon.

'Oh,' said Kate, 'but I do hate to think of you both . . . and you've only just got here . . .'

'We'll come straight back.'

'Well,' said Kate bravely, 'If you think you ought . . . You'll like the Northern Lights anyway, I must say they *are* pretty, you'll see as you cross the line . . .'

'Kate, are you crying?' asked Simon.

'Of *course* not!' said Kate, sniffing hugely. 'It's these ridiculous dragons. The smoke gets in my eyes!'

All the same she watched very anxiously as the train travelled on again without her, the

Northern Lights flashed crimson and electric blue, and the boys lost one dimension after another, until they Vanished Utterly into the dark. To her great relief they reappeared almost immediately, and rushed towards her, round eyed and flat before leaping the last black line into Dragon Land and becoming themselves again.

'Awful!' exclaimed Dougal as soon as he could speak. 'Get down, you daft dragon! Kate, make them get down! They've knocked Simon right over!'

'They should be on leads!' said Kate, tugging the largest dragon away from Simon and helping him to his feet. 'Leave Simon alone you naughty monster! A great big dragon like you!'

Just then the little train came trundling round again, newly reladen by Samuel Moon.

'Not *more* people!' groaned Kate, as with terrified faces the passengers chugged past, flashed into the blaze of the Northern Lights and then rapidly disappeared. 'How are we ever we going to get them safely back again?

Come *away* from that crack, you bad dragon! You're melting it!'

'Is he?' asked Simon, interestedly, and Dougal said suddenly, 'Make him melt it some more, Kate! Madeline's father said he thought the sections must be frozen together.'

'Don't be silly Dougal darling!' said Kate. 'If it gets any bigger goodness knows how many people might end up slipping down.'

'That's just it. They've *got* to slip down,' said Dougal. 'Don't you see Kate, that's the only way back. Everyone's got to go down that crack before morning, or they'll be packed up and taken away with the rest of the fair.'

Kate stared at him in disbelief and then stepped cautiously forwards to peer down. It looked like a long, narrow letterbox in the ice, an opening into a thousand metres of bottomless blue. Steam from the dragon's melting swirled up from the depths. She shuddered and stepped back.

'It's quite safe,' said Dougal. 'It comes out into the school playing field.'

It did not look like it came out into the

playing field. It looked like it came out into the end of the world. Simon gazed down into it and was suddenly filled with a strange, giddy urge to jump. After all, Dougal's toddlers had fallen down and come out safely, and someone had to go first.

'I'll show you, Kate,' he said, suddenly making his mind up, and stepped over the line into the second dimension, sat down, slid his legs over the crack, and let go.

'NO, SIMON!' screamed Kate, but was too late.

Simon was not very wide, but still he was wider than a two year old. He did not so much fall as ooze out of sight. His hands remained sticking up out of the ice for some time after the rest of his body had disappeared.

The dragons retreated at the strangeness of this sight, but the flat passengers in the next section hurried much closer, and behind them the exclamation marks suddenly became visible people again. In the outer darkness invisible dots became streaks of light.

Simon's hands disappeared and there followed a tense and anxious silence. How far would Simon have to fall, wondered Dougal, and did it get narrower or wider? What if Simon had got half way and then stuck? He was just preparing to get Kate to hang on to his ankles while he dived to the rescue when from behind him he heard a faint and far away hum.

'Good old Simon!' exclaimed Dougal, recognising the sound at once. 'Oh *good* old Simon! Look Kate! Stop crying and look!'

The little train was whizzing up from behind. In it, beaming with pride, sat Simon.

'Easy as pie!' he said, braking neatly beside Kate and Dougal.

'Oh Simon!' said Kate. 'Oh Simon, I thought you were lost!'

'I thought he was stuck,' said Dougal.

'That was the only bad bit,' admitted Simon. 'It's so tight a fit. It's lovely on the other side though. Still sunny . . .'

'Still sunny!' repeated Kate wonderingly, gazing at the arctic waste that surrounded them.

'Quite hot really, and everyone except Class 4b's gone home. A lot of them wanted to come back with me but Madeline said they'd better wait until we got the way out a bit bigger. She thought of a way of doing it too. I told her about the dragons and she said to throw the coconut down the crack.'

'Then what?' asked Dougal.

'Then the dragons will try and get it back again. And their firey breath will melt the ice and the crack will get much wider. And all we will have to do after that is to get everyone to line up and jump down. Madeline said it should be quite simple.'

'Madeline always thinks things should be

quite simple,' said Dougal, 'and they never are.'

'She's getting everyone to close up the other rides now,' continued Simon, 'and when the people land in the playing field she says she will just tell them kindly and politely that the fair is over and that it is time to go home . . .'

'There's *one* thing I'm worrying about,' interrupted Kate. 'No, that's not true . . . there's dozens of things I'm worrying about but one especially . . .'

'What?' asked Dougal and Simon.

'Never mind,' said Kate. 'I expect I'm being silly. I'll get the coconut.'

The coconut was retrieved (not without great difficulty) from the jaws of the dragon Kate had named Trifle. It was thrown down the crack, where it jammed, just out of reach of the dragons but still perfectly visible. The dragons stuck their heads down the crack and roared with frustration. Clouds of steam arose as the ice melted and the crack became a gaping chasm.

'Jump!' shrieked Kate. 'We don't know if it works from this side!'

A minute later and the gap would have been too wide for them, but they leapt into two dimensional flatness just in time. As they did so, the coconut became free and plopped out onto the grass below and rolled away.

Then everything became very quiet. The dragons realised that their coconut was gone and lay sulkily silent, with their heads on their front paws, gazing reproachfully at Kate from round, golden eyes. The crowds of disappeared people, seeing the dragons so quiet, and now separated from them by a large chasm, began to come closer. The bravest of them (among them the school secretary), peered cautiously over the edge. Great changes had taken place. The blue depths beneath no longer looked as if they went on for ever. Instead they clearly ended in the grass of Pudding Bag School playing field. When people saw that grass, so far away and yet so near they could not take their eyes off it, and one by one, some boldly and some

quaking, some resigned and some disbelieving, they allowed themselves to slide
down.

CHAPTER SEVEN

What Happened In The End

In the playing field of Pudding Bag School the vanished passengers of the Triple Terror Express were returning by the dozen. Some of them slid out at the side of the platform (where Dougal's toddlers had reappeared), but most of them tumbled out right underneath. They landed among the damp green grass and long shadows of a Midsummer evening. There they were helped to their feet by the waiting members of Class 4b, all of them eager to explain as kindly and politely as they knew how, that the fair was now over and it was time to go home.

The mothers of Dougal's babies, after an amazed but noiseless reunion with their sleeping angels, obeyed at once. As carefully as if they were handling unexploded bombs they lifted their offspring from the dewy grass, lowered them into buggies and tiptoed silently away.

Not so the rest of the passengers, who stood around in disconsolate groups, muttering crossly to each other and reeking of magic. As more and more people arrived the groups grew larger and larger.

'What shall we do with them?' asked Madeline anxiously. 'I thought they'd be glad to go home!'

'They seem to be waiting for something,' said Charlotte, and Samuel, after a little eavesdropping around the groups, discovered what it was. Moments later the magic words: 'Money back at the gate!' had cleared the field.

At last there was no one left to reappear except Simon and Dougal and Kate. Simon and Dougal came first and after them came Kate. And after Kate came the three dragons, Jelly and Trifle and Angel Delight.

'Bother oh bother oh bother!' said Kate. 'I

thought that might happen!'

Luckily the dragons, like everything else that belonged to the Triple Terror Express, were far larger on the inside than on the outside. On the outside they were the size of rather large cats.

'Rather large, rather green, rather scaley, rather hot cats!' said Kate crossly as they rolled at her feet.

'Look Father, dragons!' said Madeline, waking Professor Brown to show him the latest arrivals.

Professor Brown stared closely at Jelly and Trifle and Angel Delight and said Very Quaint, but he doubted they actually existed.

'Pure myth,' he explained, rubbing the scorch mark that Jelly had made on his trouser leg. 'Pure myth!' And, carefully avoiding squashing a clump of daisies, he lay back to study the constellations of midsummer stars that were beginning to appear in the sky.

'She loves me, she loves me not . . .' Madeline heard him murmuring. He was a most impractical man.

As soon as Dougal had landed and had thanked his friends and apologized to the moose and had patted the green grass as if he loved it, he said,

'We must put the Triple Terror Express back exactly like it was and then no one will ever know that anything has happened.'

'What about the dragons?' asked Kate.

'I wonder if it's still frozen up,' said Samuel.

Madeline, who was as practical as her father was not, said that if it was they could use the dragons as blow torches to unfreeze it. This plan worked perfectly, and in very little time the first section was loose enough for Dougal to get his fingers in and turn the controls back to their original settings, Icy Cavern from 'Max' to 'Min', Darkness from 'Utter and Complete' to 'Simulated', Northern Lights from 'Main' to 'Back Up', and the Dragons from 'Live' to 'Illustrated'.

'Perhaps it takes a few minutes to work on the dragons,' said Kate, looking at Jelly, Trifle and Angel Delight who remained quite obviously and hotly 'Live'.

It worked on everything else however. After the controls had been changed it took hardly any time to free the sections completely. Inside there was no trace at all of the icy wilderness. It was not even particularly dark. There was, however, the most tremendous smell of magic. It came billowing out like bonfire smoke, saturating the hair and clothes of Class 4b, as well as the fur of the moose.

'Personally I think it's rather nice,' said Kate, 'but it'll be a dead give away, Dougal darling, if anyone comes sniffing round in the morning.'

'It will have blown away by then,' replied Dougal comfortably, as he slotted the last section of the Triple Terror Express back into its original, uninteresting place. 'There! Finished! Just like it was!'

'Except for the dragons,' said Kate.

'We'll put the dragons in one of the carriages and buzz them through now,' said Dougal.

This turned out to be much easier said than

done. The dragons, clearly not wishing to be buzzed through and turned back into mere illustrations, made themselves very difficult to catch and hold. When caught and tied up in school sweatshirts to stop them escaping, they scorched themselves free. When lured into a stationary carriage with the remains of the coconut they exploded out again like three green rockets the moment the 'GO' button was pressed. Dawn came, and the dragons were still as 'Live' as ever, but Class 4b were exhausted.

'I wonder if you could just take them home Madeline dear,' said Kate at last. 'Since your father does not believe in them he will probably not notice them around.'

This seemed to be the only solution, Class 4b sighed with relief and went home, arriving just in time to stop their families (all of whom were only just recovered from their own experiences on the Triple Terror Express), from calling the police. The dragons, however, refused to go with Madeline. They doubled back in pursuit of Kate halfway down

Pudding Bag Lane and she was forced to take them home after all.

'What will people say?' she asked, but she need not have worried. Most people it seemed, did not believe in dragons, it was not just Madeline's father. During the time they spent with Kate the dragons were hardly noticed at all, and when they were they were described in one of the following ways:

The chameleons

The central heating

Kate's latest craze

Those green cat things with hot tongues

It's amazing what rubbish they can sell these days.

The morning after the school summer fair was a Saturday. Dougal, who had been chased up to bed by his bewildered mother at dawn, sneaked out again as soon as he could, and crept up the lane to Pudding Bag School. There he hid behind the dustbins and watched as the green and black lorries arrived, and as the Carousel, the Helter Skelter, the Dodgems and the Triple Terror Express were dismantled and loaded and driven away. He saw them go with a mixture of sadness and relief, and afterwards he went and hugged Sir Lancelot, who also looked lonely.

'We'll probably never see them again,' he said. 'No more magic.'

Sir Lancelot said nothing, but he stood quite still and let Dougal bury his nose in his neck and a strong and comforting smell of magic still clung to his fur.

The smell was still there on Monday morning, when a combination of hairwashing and clothes changing, and swimming and baths had almost completely removed it from Class 4b. Also on Monday a letter arrived from Miss Gilhoolie. She wrote that she hoped they were being Perfectly Good, and had had a happy time at the fair and had made lots of money and won the Class Prize. Also that she was very much better and would be with them again before the end of the week.

'Oh!' said Samantha, when the letter had been read aloud by Madeline. 'Oh Madeline! I forgot all about the Class Prize! It was all so lovely and magicky! I didn't charge anyone anything all the time I was looking after the Helter Skelter.'

'Me neither,' chimed in voice after voice.

'I remembered,' said Madeline, 'but it didn't seem fair, we were having so many free rides ourselves.'

'Dougal charged,' said Samuel, 'but I'm afraid I had to give it all back at the gates. I'm really sorry Doug!'

'Doesn't matter,' said Dougal. 'What else could you do? And I've still got these left!' And he waved in the air the five five pound notes pressed on him by the toddlers' mothers.

The smell that wafted from the five pound notes reminded Class 4b of another problem.

'If Miss Gilhoolie gets a whiff of Sir Lancelot like he is she'll know there's been something up,' said Simon Percy. 'You can smell him as soon as you come through the gate.'

'Perhaps he'll get rained on before she comes back,' suggested Madeline, and Class 4b watched the weather forecast very hopefully that night, and it gave a countrywide drought.

All through the school that morning classes were adding up takings, deducting expenses and working out their profits for the school summer fair. Somehow the fact that Class 4b had only raised twenty-five pounds had already leaked out. This news was greeted with howls of laughter, especially from Class 4a, who with hard work and no magic had achieved six hundred and ninety seven.

'Still, it's better than nothing at all,' Dougal said, and began to feel quite proud at having saved Class 4b from complete and utter disgrace.

Then morning break came, and Sir Lancelot was smelling as strongly of magic as ever, and nothing but drought was forecast and Madeline said, 'We must wash him,' and no one disagreed.

They washed him that lunch time with buckets of water from the girls' cloakroom, explaining truthfully to the school secretary who came out to investigate, that Sir Lancelot was feeing rather hot.

The water only seemed to make the smell of magic stronger.

'Shampoo?' suggested Emma.

'It'll have to be proper moose shampoo,' said Madeline, who knew how important it was to always wash animals with the correct shampoos. 'There's a pet shop near Regent's Park that sells everything. We'd better go tonight.'

That night a wicked little woman with yellow eyes sold them her smallest-sized bottle of moose shampoo, and the next day Class 4b handed in their profits and accounts to the school secretary.

They ran as thus:

Class 4b Accounts for School Summer Fair

Takings (after various refunds)   £25.00
Expenses (moose shampoo)   £24.95
Profit   5p

After the profits and accounts had been handed in Class 4b spent every free moment shampooing Sir Lancelot, and by Thursday morning when Miss Gilhoolie returned they had almost succeeded in getting rid of the smell of magic completely. But not utterly. Miss Gilhoolie sniffed him and looked at him and sniffed him again and said,

'Are you *sure* you've been behaving yourselves?'

Class 4b assured her that they had.

Later that day she found a bundle of screwed up photographs of people cowering in a little train while dragons roamed an arctic landscape and she said,

'Who would like to tell me about these?'

A deathly silence followed this question.

Then the results of the Class Competition were announced, and Class 4a were revealed to have beaten them by a clear margin of £696.95.

'How is it you did so badly?' asked Miss Gilhoolie. 'And how can you possibly account for Moose Shampoo as a necessary expense?'

Class 4b were saved from having to reply by a knock on the door and the arrival of the school secretary. She held out an enormous green and yellow envelope addressed in very curly, very twirly, very black writing.

'Special delivery Miss Gilhoolie, dear,' she panted, 'So I brought it along straight away.'

Miss Gilhoolie opened the envelope when the secretary had gone and inside was a brief but furious note saying Three Items had Been Discovered Missing which if not returned immediately would bring about Unfortunate but Drastic Consequences.

'What does this mean?' demanded Miss Gilhoolie, and this time everyone could honestly say they did not know, until Samantha asked brightly,

'Oh, could it be the dragons?'

Then the whole story was dragged from Class 4b.

The first thing to do was to avoid the Unfortunate but Drastic Consequences, and Dougal was sent scurrying home for the three missing items at once. They were discovered under Kate's bed, quite damp and steamy, weeping over a switched off hairdryer which they obviously assumed was dead. They were sent off straight away by special courier summoned by Miss Gilhoolie in a green and yellow fireproof box.

Then Miss Gilhoolie said, 'You should never have had that train. It was ordered by mistake. I would never have sent you anything so dangerous. But all the same, didn't you know that fair was magic? 'Didn't it *look* magic? Didn't it *act* magic? Didn't it *smell* magic?'

'Yes,' said everyone.

'Didn't I tell you never to interfere with anything that smells of magic?' demanded Miss Gilhoolie. 'Didn't I say enjoy it, but never, ever, ever interfere? Didn't I even make the smell of magic for you, so that you would be quite sure?'

'Yes,' said everyone again, and Dougal stood up and said very bravely,

'It wasn't them, Miss Gilhoolie. It was me. It was running like clockwork until I changed it. It was all my fault.'

'I might have known,' said Miss Gilhoolie crossly, and then she said, less crossly. 'Oh well, I suppose if you don't learn one way, you'll learn another.'

'I've learnt now,' said Dougal.

'You've lost the Special Class Prize though,' said Miss Gilhoolie. 'Class 4a will get it now. It is a trip to Alton Towers. All rides free. I'm glad you find that funny Dougal McDougal!'

'It would never have been so good as your

fair,' said Dougal. 'Miss Gilhoolie?'

'Well, what?'

'Can we go out and sniff the moose?'

'Sniff the moose?'

'Just to remind us.'

'Just to remind you?'

'Of the smell of magic.'

'I don't see why not,' said Miss Gilhoolie.

The school secretary looked out of her window at Class 4b and she thought,

'Natural History again! Dear children! Dear Miss Gilhoolie! How very happy they seem to have her back!'